MRS PIG
GETS CROSS

Also by Mary Rayner

Mr and Mrs Pig's Evening Out
Garth Pig and the Icecream Lady
Mrs Pig's Bulk Buy
One by One
Ten Pink Piglets
Wicked William

This edition first published in 1996 by
Macmillan Children's Books
a division of Macmillan Publishers Ltd,
25 Eccleston Place, London SW1W 9NF
and Basingstoke
Associated companies worldwide

ISBN 0 333 63750 X (hardback)
ISBN 0 333 64498 0 (paperback)

Mrs Pig Gets Cross first appeared in *Cricket Magazine*,
February 1979, under the title of *Mrs Pig Gives Up*.

Text and illustrations copyright © Mary Rayner 1986, 1996

The right of Mary Rayner to be identified as the author of this work has been
asserted by her in accordance with the Copyright Designs and Patents Act 1988.

1 3 5 7 9 8 6 4 2

A CIP catalogue record for this book is available from the British Library

Printed in Hong Kong

MRS PIG GETS CROSS

Written and illustrated by
Mary Rayner

Macmillan Children's Books

There once lived a family of pigs. There was Father Pig and Mother Pig, and then there were ten piglets. The eldest was Sorrel Pig. Then came Bryony, then Hilary, Sarah, Toby,

Cindy, William and Alun, and finally the two smallest, Benjamin and Garth.

One day Mrs Pig was picking up the toys strewn all over the kitchen floor. She grunted angrily. She hated bending because she was so stout. After picking up several more toys she straightened up and banged them down on the table.

"I am not going to do any more. You are the most untidy piglets I know. Your things can just *stay* lying about. I am too tired to do it for you," she said.

The ten piglets helped a bit. Some bricks were thrown into the brick bin.

The railway that twined its way under and round
and through the kitchen chairs was broken in pieces,
but somehow it did not all get as far as its box.

When Mr Pig came home after a late evening he found the house messier than ever. He stepped over Garth Pig's tricycle in the hall and then over Toby's rocket, glanced at the piles of coats, bags, papers and boots that lay on the stairs, and went into the living room. Mrs Pig was lying on the sofa with a magazine.

"Why can't you make the children clear up themselves?" grumbled Mr Pig. "They should put away their own toys and clothes."

Mrs Pig said she hadn't felt up to getting them to do it.
Then she and Mr Pig began to argue about whose turn it
was to make the tea, and in the end they went to bed
without any. Father Pig was so put out that he forgot to
lock the front door.

Halfway through the night, when the house was in darkness, a foxy-looking fellow came sneaking up the street. It was a burglar. He tried all the doors until he came to Mr and Mrs Pig's house.

Their door opened easily.

The burglar crept in. There was a light on right at the top of the stairs, but down in the hall it was pitch dark. He took a few steps forward and banged straight into Garth's tricycle. *Ow* – he clapped a paw over his mouth to stop himself crying out.

He tiptoed on. *Crash!* Into Toby's rocket. On he went. *Blap!* On to William's boot on the bottom step. He got up. *Oops!* Sarah's satchel strap nearly sent him flying. He staggered on, up the stairs towards what he thought must be the grown-ups' room.

He opened the door. Both were asleep. He crept round the bed to the dressing-table and silently, silently slid open the drawers. Mrs Pig kept all *her* things exactly where they should be. The burglar emptied her jewellery into a little bag and then went over to the bedside table. He found Mr Pig's wallet laid neatly beside his loose change, and took them both.

The noise of falling pieces of rocket had slightly woken Mr Pig. Now he stirred in his sleep and gave a grunt.

The burglar fled.

He ran lightly down the first few stairs – and fell headlong over William's other boot, dropping everything as he somersaulted down.

He picked himself up and felt about for the bag and the wallet. Ah, something soft. No, William's sock. Then he found the bag. Empty. Everything had shot out.

A faint thump seemed to come from overhead. Feverishly the burglar groped about. He found some small knobbly things which he stuffed into the bag, and something squarish, which felt like a wallet. He took it and ran out of the house.

When he reached a street lamp, the burglar took out the wallet to count the money. It wasn't a wallet at all. It was the holder for Sorrel's old bus pass, which she had left lying on the hall floor. He threw it down.

Then he opened the bag and emptied it into his paw. Out came about twenty pieces of Lego.

The burglar jumped up and down with rage and went home a sadder and a wiser fellow.

And in case you are thinking that this story tells you never to put your things away in their proper places, it does not. It says: Be careful not to make your mother and father so cross that they forget to bolt the doors.

Other Macmillan picture books you will enjoy

Sweetie	Jonathan Allen
The Nodland Express	Anna Clarke and Martin Rowson
Martha Speaks	Susan Meddaugh
The Foxbury Force and the Pirates	Graham Oakley
The Barnyard Band	Jim Riordan and Charles Fuge
Mudge the Smuggler	John Ryan
Grampa Goes West	Selina Young

For a complete list of titles, write to

Macmillan Children's Books
25, Eccleston Place
London SW1W 9NF